'You do look much bigger than you did yesterday,' said Dad. 'But where will you go?'

'I haven't decided yet,' said Audrey.

So Dad and Audrey went outside to look.

'How about here?' said Dad.

'Way too small,' said Audrey.

A HOUSE of HER OWN

by Jenny Hughes
illustrated by Jonathan Bentley

LITTLE HARE
www.littleharebooks.com

'Your house is getting too small for me,'
said Audrey one morning.

'What about here?' asked Dad.

'It's far too big,' said Audrey.

'Or here?'

'It's too crowded,' Audrey said.
'Let's build a house up there!'

'It's very high,' said Dad.

'Almost as high as the sky,' said Audrey.
'But I'm bigger than I was yesterday.'

So Audrey and her dad went to see what they could find.

'First I'll need a staircase,' said Audrey.
'With a banister so I can slide from the top.'

Dad built a staircase.

'And somewhere I can play,
with a bathtub for snorkelling.'

Dad built a place to play.

'And somewhere to sip tea,' said Audrey.
'And a cupboard to hide the dirty cups.'

Dad made somewhere
to sip tea.

'A blue bed would be nice,' said Audrey.
'So I can keep my secrets underneath.'

Dad made a bed.

'Now I need a chair for every guest.'

Dad made chairs.

'And don't forget a stove so I can cook cakes,
and lick the bowl clean.'

Dad made a stove.

'It's a very high house,' said Dad.

'Almost as high as the sky,' said Audrey.
'But I'm much bigger than I was yesterday.'

'Well, goodnight, my darling,'
said Dad as he tidied his tools.
'Don't stay up late.'

Audrey's tummy turned over.

'I haven't got my fluffy blanket,' she said.

'You can borrow my jumper,' said Dad
as he walked down the staircase.

Audrey sniffed.

'I think I've caught a cold,' she said.
'I might sneeze the leaves off the tree.'

Dad headed up the path. 'You can rake them up
in the morning,' he said.

Audrey's knees trembled.

'But I've eaten the cakes,' she said.
'My tummy might grumble and wake the birds.'

'Birds don't mind waking early,' said Dad
as he passed the pond.

'But what if it rains in the night?' Audrey said.
'I might wash away in a flood!'

'I know where there's a staircase,' said Dad.

'Do you?' said Audrey.

'It leads to a place safe and warm,' said Dad.

'Does it?' said Audrey.

'There's soup for two and two snug beds.
You can always come home with me.'

'Are you sure?' asked Audrey.

'Very sure,' said Dad.

'Even if I'm bigger than I was yesterday?' said Audrey.

'Even if you're twice as big as you were yesterday,' said Dad.

'For as long as I like?' asked Audrey.

'Even longer,' said Dad.

Audrey ran up the path, and together
they climbed the steps to the house...

that wasn't too small at all.

For Ivy, Freya, Katie and Margrete—JH

For Ruby—JB

Little Hare Books
an imprint of
Hardie Grant Egmont
Ground Floor, Building 1, 658 Church Street
Richmond, Victoria 3121, Australia

www.littleharebooks.com

First published 2014
First published in paperback 2014

Cataloguing-in-Publication details are available from the
National Library of Australia

9781760121471 (pbk.)

Designed by Vida & Luke Kelly
Produced by Pica Digital, Singapore
Printed through Asia Pacific Offset
Printed in Shenzhen, Guangdong Province, China

5 4 3 2 1

The illustrations in this book were created using watercolours,
pencil and scanned textures.